# Yetsa's Sweater

# Yetsa's Sweater

Sylvia Olsen

Illustrated by

Joan Larson

sononis PRESS

WINLAW, BRITISH COLUMBIA

Library and Archives Canada Cataloguing in Publication

Olsen, Sylvia, 1955-
    Yetsa's sweater / Sylvia Olsen ; illustrated by Joan Larson.

ISBN 1-55039-155-0

    1. Coast Salish Indians—Juvenile fiction.  2. Picture books for children.

I. Larson, Joan  II. Title.

PS8579.L728Y47 2006          jC813'.6          C2006-904024-9

First printing September 2006
Second printing September 2007

Sono Nis Press most gratefully acknowledges support for our publishing program provided by the Government of Canada through the Book Publishing Industry Development Program (BPIDP) and the Canada Council for the Arts, and by the Province of British Columbia through the British Columbia Arts Council and the Book Publishing Tax Credit, Ministry of Provincial Revenue.

Edited by Laura Peetoom
Copy edited by Dawn Loewen
Cover and interior design by Jim Brennan

Published by
SONO NIS PRESS
Box 160
Winlaw, BC  V0G 2J0
1-800-370-5228

books@sononis.com
www.sononis.com

Distributed in the U.S. by
Orca Book Publishers
Box 468
Custer, WA  98240-0468
1-800-210-5277

The Canada Council | Le Conseil des Arts
for the Arts | du Canada

Printed and bound in Canada by Friesens Printing

For Laura Olsen and May Sam
and the other Coast Salish knitters
who have created the beautiful
Cowichan sweaters

It's a bright Saturday in May. Yetsa and her mom walk down the road, through the oak trees, and along the trail to Grandma's house.

Grandma lives near the beach and it's chilly when the wind blows off the salt water. Yetsa wears her favourite sweater. It's too small for her, but she doesn't care. Yetsa has had it since she was little. It's toasty warm. It has waves and flowers and tiny salmon designs on it. Grandma knit it for her.

"Your sweater tells a story about your family," Grandma always says. "I knit flowers on the sweater because your mom loves her garden. I knit salmon on the sleeves because your dad loves fishing. And I knit waves around the bottom because you love the beach."

Yetsa loves her sweater. She loves Saturdays. And she loves to go to Grandma's house to help her prepare wool.

Grandma is out in the back adding sticks of fir and alder and maple wood to the fire. A round-bellied pot sits on a grate over the fire. The outside of the pot is covered with black soot. The pot is so big, Yetsa could climb in and have a bath. It's filled with water now—but it's the wool that's going to have a bath, not Yetsa. Farmer McNutt has sheared his sheep and brought all his fleeces to Grandma.

"Can I help?" Yetsa calls.

Grandma holds her arms
open and welcomes Yetsa.

"I've been waiting for you,"
she says.

The bundles of fleece are piled almost as high as Grandma: black fleeces, white fleeces, and fleeces in different shades of grey. Grandma and Mom untie the bundles, shake the fleeces, and lay them on the grass.

Yetsa knows just what to do. She follows behind and pulls hay, prickles, and twigs out of the wool, tossing them into the fire. She reaches into a black fleece and pulls out a thick handful of dirt—at least, she thinks it's dirt.

"Yuck, yuck, yuck!" she hollers, shaking her hand like crazy. "Sheep poop!"

Grandma and Mom laugh, and Grandma says, "That old farmer McNutt—he's supposed to leave that stuff on the farm."

"This is the ucky-yuckiest part of the whole job," says Yetsa.

Grandma checks the fleeces for any more sheep poop while Yetsa cleans her hand. Then Yetsa and Mom get back to work pulling the rest of the barnyard mess out of the wool.

When they are done, Grandma chooses a big white fleece and stuffs it into the hot water. She pours soap over the wool and gently stirs the pot with a long wooden pole.

"It looks like a witch's stew," laughs Yetsa as she watches steam rise into the air.

Grandma fills two more pots with cold water for rinsing. She stirs the washing pot a few more times, then lifts the wool with her stick and places it in the rinse water. The wool is heavy and hot. Mom gets a stick and helps her.

"Now for my favourite part," Yetsa says.

Yetsa sinks her hands into the cold water to feel it turn warm from the hot washed wool. She swishes the long strands of wool around. She presses the brownish bits of the wool between her fingers and watches them turn white in the clean rinse water. She pulls big clumps of clean wool out of the water and dumps them into the final rinsing pot.

When Grandma says the rinse is finished, they pull the wool out of the pot and twist it and twist it and twist it until all the water is squeezed out. Yetsa's little hands have a hard time wringing out the heavy wool. By the time she is ready to hang the wool on the lines, water is running down her arms, under her arms, and down her legs.

"Look at yourself, girl!" Mom exclaims. "I'm going to have to wring *you* out and hang *you* on the line."

Yetsa feels cold and wet, but she is happy to see the freshly washed clumps of wool hanging in the sun and swishing in the spring breeze. Her stomach growls.

"Time for some fresh bread and blackberry jam," says Grandma.

"Yum!" says Yetsa. Grandma's homemade blackberry jam is one of her favourite foods.

After their snack Yetsa and Mom say goodbye.

"See you bright and early next Saturday!" Grandma hollers as they walk up the path. "We have a lot of work to do."

Yetsa and Mom arrive before
nine o'clock the following
Saturday morning. Grandma
is already outside, sitting
on a lawn chair behind a
mountain of white wool.
Clean and dry, the wool
looks ten times bigger
than it did before.

"Grandma, it looks like
a big woolly cloud
fell out of the sky and
landed in your yard!"
laughs Yetsa.

Yetsa and Mom sit down beside Grandma. They each take a clump of wool from the cloud mountain and begin to pull the strands apart. The wool gets even fluffier.

"Why is it called teasing when we pull the wool to make it fluffy?" asks Yetsa.

"I don't know," says Grandma. "I asked the same question when I was a girl and no one knew the answer."

When they have a pile of teased wool, Grandma starts up the carding machine. It looks like two of the biggest hairbrushes Yetsa has ever seen, only much more dangerous. Grandma doesn't let her go near the machine when it is running. Yetsa doesn't mind. She wouldn't want to get her fingers caught in the big bristly metal tubes.

Yetsa hands Grandma some teased wool, and Grandma feeds it into the machine. She pulls the carded wool off the machine with a long needle. It is soft and flat, with no knots or tangles.

"Just like freshly brushed hair," says Yetsa.

"And ready to spin," nods Grandma.

"Can I help? Can I help?" pleads Yetsa. But she knows the answer. Spinning is a hard job. The spinner is big, and Grandma has to use her hands and her feet at the same time to make it work. Once when Grandma wasn't looking Yetsa tried to spin, but the wool got tangled around the machine so badly that Grandma had to break it off and throw it away.

"You can help by feeding me the wool," says Grandma, "and when you are older and bigger I'll teach you to use the spinning machine."

Yetsa is very hungry after helping with teasing, carding, and spinning. Her arms hurt and her fingers are tired from pulling and pulling and pulling. The blackberry jam and fresh bread taste scrumptious.

When Yetsa and Mom arrive the next Saturday, Grandma isn't in the backyard. She is sitting in her living room on her favourite rocking chair. Stacked on either side of her in big cedar-root baskets are balls and balls of woollen yarn. There is black yarn, white yarn, and yarn in different shades of grey, wound as big as soccer balls.

"You've been busy!" says Yetsa.

"I sure have been, Yetsa," says Grandma. "I haven't stopped
spinning since last Saturday. Now I'm ready for the winter.
I have enough wool to knit many, many sweaters."

Yetsa sits next to Grandma and watches her needles flick together, so fast she can't keep track. She closes her eyes and listens: *clickety, clickety, click.* Then she opens her eyes again and studies the white and black wool descending from the needles in a beautiful design.

"What are you knitting into this sweater, Grandma?"
Yetsa asks.

Grandma smiles.

"Flowers. Whales and waves. Woolly clouds, and
blackberries."

## The Cowichan Sweater

Coast Salish women have been knitting the beautiful Cowichan sweaters for more than a hundred years. Yetsa, the author's granddaughter, is in the sixth generation of a family of Coast Salish knitters. Her aunt, grandmother, grandfather (yes, some men knit the sweaters too), great-grandmother, and great-great-grandmother have all made these sweaters.

In the late 19th century, Scottish settlers came to British Columbia and introduced Coast Salish women to the art of knitting. The women were already skilled and artful woolworkers, having woven Coast Salish blankets for centuries. The knitted sweaters the women quickly learned to make became known as Cowichan sweaters, largely because the Cowichan were the most populated tribe in the region. Children as young as five and six began to learn the craft of sweater-making, as Yetsa did in the story, by helping to prepare wool. Once the children reached eight or nine they were often given their own sets of needles and taught to make hats and socks. Gradually, as the children grew and became more skilful, they took on larger garments. Spinning, thought to be the most difficult task in making the sweaters, was often learned in one's early twenties.

During the 1950s and 1960s, Cowichan sweaters became widely known and favoured outerwear and were exported to many foreign countries. In the 1970s they became a fashion statement, especially loved in Japan. The sweater industry doubled and tripled in size. Coast Salish women worked feverishly to fill foreign orders. Unfortunately, after a few decades, sales plummeted and the sweaters were largely replaced by polar fleece and other synthetic fibres—as fashion comes, so it goes.

Still, the Cowichan sweater remains a treasured West Coast garment. The lanolin-laden wool makes the sweaters resistant to wind and rain. The distinctive designs make them beautiful and unique. These designs have no single origin. Some are purely decorative, while others represent flowers, waves, cockleshells, or animals such as eagles and deer. Knitters often have favourite designs they learned from their grandparents and have developed a distinctive, recognizable style of knitting.

Only a few Coast Salish knitters produce the sweaters today. Laura Olsen, Yetsa's great-grandmother, is still knitting beautiful sweaters at ninety years of age. Cowichan sweaters no longer play the important role they once did in Coast Salish economy or society, but they are still available in specialty shops. If you buy a sweater, check that it is a genuine article made by a Coast Salish person.